IF YOU EVER MEET ZACHARY
RUTHLESS, YOU MIGHT JUST THINK
HE'S THE NICEST TEN-YEAR-OLD
BOY IN THE WORLD. HIS MOUTH
NATURALLY CURVES INTO A SMALL
SMILE. HIS EYES ARE BRIGHT AND
WIDE. HE BLINKS A LOT, AND
EVERYONE KNOWS PEOPLE WHO
ARE GOOD AND KIND AND
SWEET BLINK A LOT.

BUT DON'T BE FOOLED.
YOU CAN'T ALWAYS JUDGE
A BOOK BY ITS COVER.

THE ROTTEN ADVENTURES OF Zachary Ruthless

THE ROTTEN ADVENTURES OF Zachary Ruthless

ALLAN WOODROW

Illustrated by
AARON BLECHA

HARPER
An Imprint of HarperCollinsPublishers

Library of Congress Cataloging-in-Publication Data
Woodrow, Allan.
The rotten adventures of Zachary Ruthless / by Allan
Woodrow ; [illustrated by Aaron Blecha]. — 1st ed.
      p.   cm. — (The rotten adventures of Zachary
Ruthless ; #1)
Summary: Ten-year-old Zachary Ruthless, who aspires
to join the Society of Utterly Rotten, Beastly, and Loathsome
Lawbreaking Scoundrels (SOURBALLS), acquires an inex-
perienced but earnest henchman and sets out to prove how
evil he can be.
ISBN 978-0-06-200587-8
[1. Behavior—Fiction.   2. Humorous stories.]   I. Blecha,
Aaron, ill.   II. Title.
PZ7.W86047Ro   2011   2010040427
[Fic]—dc22   CIP
                                               AC

Typography by Erin Fitzsimmons
11 12 13 14 15   CG/CW   10 9 8 7 6 5 4 3 2 1
❖
First Edition

To Lauren. We did it! Bwa-ha-ha!
—A. W.

For Tate the Great
—A. B.

Acknowledgments

I'd like to thank all the people both rotten and not so rotten who helped bring Zachary's story to light. You fools! To Lauren, for your heart. To Madelyn and Emmy, for your inspiration. To Mom and Dad, for, well, everything. To Brenda Ferber, Jenny Meyerhoff, and the gang at the North Shore Writers Studio, for your encouragement. To my agent Joanna Volpe, for your guidance, and to my editor, Maria Gomez, and everyone at HarperCollins, for letting Zachary hypnotize you into publishing this thing, um, I mean, for your vision. But most of all, to Stanley the Invisible Squirrel, who lives in my desk drawer and comes out at night, types stories, and then lets me take all the credit.

CONTENTS

1

★ 💀 ★

BWA-HA-HA!

Zachary Ruthless tightened his grip around the snake he had found lurking in the bushes below his tree fort that morning. No one was watching him. Perfect. He slipped the snake into Mrs. Snyder's mailbox.

"Bwa-ha-ha!" he cackled. Zachary knew every self-respecting rotten evildoer needs a gleeful, evil cackle.

1

S-S-S-S-S

But although he practiced almost every day, his cackle needed work. It sounded like a hyena with the hiccups.

Zachary continued walking past the two-story houses along his street, and then turned into Plentyville's small downtown. He read the sign on the side of the road:

But Zachary knew plenty of bad things also happened in Plentyville.

In fact, he made sure of it.

The warm sun shone overhead, and birds chirped merrily in the trees. Zachary frowned. He needed to do something rotten. Fast.

Zachary made a mental list of terrible things he could do:

2. Turn rainbows into fiery death balls

3. Melt the state capitol with a giant microwave oven

1. Alter the gravity of the earth so it crashes into Pluto

WELCOME TO PLUTO

He particularly liked the last idea, but didn't know where he could find a microwave oven big enough. Of course, turning rainbows into death balls or altering Earth's gravity was tricky, too. Maybe someday. A guy's got to have dreams, right?

Across the street, a giant inflatable fish stood outside the Plentyville Seafood Shop. Next to the store was Big Al's Hot Dog Emporium, with a giant truck of mustard parked outside.

Zachary rubbed his hands together as he hatched an evil scheme. This would be as easy as stealing candy from a baby, or even easier since it was hard to find a baby with candy to steal. They usually just had rattles and things covered in spit.

From the side of the store, Zachary carefully unlatched the end of the hose leading from the air tank into the fish. He then attached it to a spigot on the side of the mustard truck. He twisted the valve.

Now all he had to do was wait. And leave. Quickly.

Zachary turned to escape and bumped into Amanda Goodbar.

She stood in his way, her hands on her hips. "What are you doing?"

Amanda and Zachary had been in class together last year. Not seeing the nosy goody two-shoes Amanda Goodbar was one of the perks of summer vacation.

"Nothing," said Zachary. He tried to walk around her, but she sidestepped in front of him.

"You're up to something," she said. Zachary opened his eyes wide and blinked rapidly.

"You can't fool me with your blinking eyes," said Amanda. "I'm onto you." Amanda never blinked a lot. Her dark hair hung limply on her head. Her eyebrows narrowed and her forehead wrinkled. Unlike Zachary, she always looked like she was up to no good, but Zachary knew better. She was always up to good.

Zachary looked behind him. The inflatable fish was already starting to expand, with little bits of mustard bubbling out of its mouth. "Um, can we talk on the other side of the street?"

"No way, Ruthless," said Amanda, staring right at Zachary. "Right before summer vacation started someone put a box of spiders in my locker at school. I know it was you."

"How do you know that?"

"A note on the box said 'This is the property of Zachary Ruthless.'" Zachary knew he should have checked that box more carefully before filling it with bugs.

He fidgeted.

Mustard oozed out of the fish's eyes and gills. The inflatable balloon was bursting at the seams.

"It wasn't me. It must have

8

been another Zachary Ruthless." Zachary blinked faster.

"Blink all you want, buster. You might have everyone fooled, but not me."

Zachary could hear the creaking sounds of the latex fish stretching and stretching.

"Sorry, I have to run!" Zachary was small and fast. He ducked past the outstretched arms of Amanda, and was already in the street when he heard . . .

KA-POW!

A spurt of mustard landed on Zachary's foot. He looked up. The inflatable fish was gone and in its place was a giant mustard swamp. Amanda was completely covered

in mustard, thick
yellow puddles
dripping from her
head to her toes.

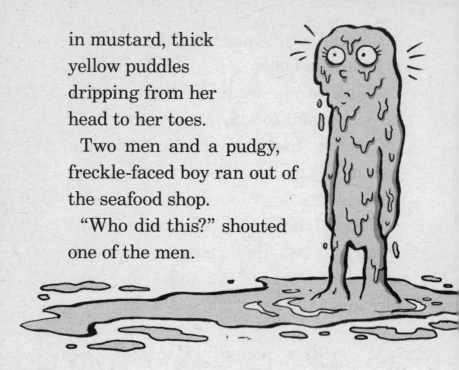

Two men and a pudgy,
freckle-faced boy ran out of
the seafood shop.

"Who did this?" shouted
one of the men.

"There's the culprit!" shouted the
other. He pointed to Amanda.

Zachary watched as one of the men
grabbed her arms. He heard him say,
"You're in big trouble, girl."

"But it wasn't me!" said Amanda. "It
was him!" she pointed to Zachary.

The men looked over. Zachary blinked.

"Nice try," the man said to Amanda. "But you're only making it worse for yourself."

Next to them, the pudgy, freckle-faced boy looked at Zachary. Their eyes met. The kid smiled and waved. Zachary ignored him, turned, and began walking away.

"I'll get you for this, Ruthless!" screamed Amanda, but Zachary was already halfway down the street, a wide grin on his face.

2

★ 💀 ★

GOOD
SAMARITAN
SCHOOL

Zachary sat at the dinner table, his plate empty except for some mashed potatoes and hidden under them, uneaten, his broccoli. His parents didn't notice. They were too nice to suspect Zachary was ever up to no good.

His mother, Ruthy Ruthless, was short, plump, and had a smile that shone as brightly as a Christmas tree. It was a marvelous smile, if you liked that sort of thing, which Zachary didn't.

"I baked a treat," she said, holding out a tray of sugar cookies in the shapes of hearts. Zachary took one, though eating a heart-shaped cookie didn't feel right. He broke it in half. Eating a broken heart seemed better.

Zachary's dad, Willard Ruthless, took a cookie, too. He had kind eyes and a kind mouth and two hairs on his bald but kind head.

Zachary shivered. How could he possibly be related to such good people?

As Zachary chewed, he glanced at the pink walls

of the house and the bunny rabbit knickknacks sitting on the counters. It was a miracle Zachary could keep his food down.

"We're worried about you." His dad interrupted Zachary's thoughts.

"Me?" Zachary blinked quickly.

"There are bad influences in town," said his mom. "Did you hear Amanda Goodbar splattered the Plentyville Seafood Shop with a condiment the other day?"

Zachary resisted the urge to cackle.

"And we heard someone in your school put spiders in your teacher's lunch box and boxes of snakes in some of the school lockers."

"It's the other way around," said Zachary. "The snakes went in the lunch box and the spiders went in the lockers. But I guess your way works, too."

His parents looked at him.

"I mean, if you dared do such a despicable act." Zachary opened his eyes wide and blinked again. His parents smiled.

Zachary's dad held out a brochure.

"We're sending you to Good Samaritan School this summer."

Zachary didn't like the sound of that one bit. "What's that?"

"Good Samaritan School is a summer school for good boys and girls who eat their broccoli and never think rotten thoughts. Like you."

Zachary couldn't speak. A lump entered his throat and began expanding faster than a mustard-filled fish balloon.

"Not everyone is as good-hearted as you are, sweetiekins," said his mom. "At Sister Celia's School for Good Samaritans you'll be around students as sweet and lovable as you are every minute of every day."

Zachary's dad handed him the brochure,

but Zachary didn't want to touch it. He was afraid he'd catch goodness, like you'd catch a cold or worms.

"You'll love it." His dad smiled.

Zachary stared in horror at the pamphlet. On the cover, the boys wore ties. The girls wore skirts. Everyone looked so happy.

Zachary shivered.

The pictures inside were even worse. A boy helped a little old lady across the street. A girl enjoyed a plate of vegetables for lunch. Kids stood in a line, single file, waiting their turns to pet a puppy. Evil people hate puppies. You can look it up.

18

Zachary's head spun and his stomach felt queasy.

"Are you okay?" said his mom. "You look a little green."

"I think I'm going to be sick," he sputtered. Zachary ran to the bathroom down the hall, opening the lid of the toilet just in time.

3

SOURBALLS

The next day Zachary sat on the dirty, dusty, and grimy floor of his tree fort, his evil grin growing wider and his eyebrows scrunching in a particularly rotten way. His hands trembled as he read the advertisement in the back of *Super Villain Weekly* once again:

Are You Up to No Good?
The Society of Utterly Rotten, Beastly,

and Loathsome Lawbreaking Scoundrels (SOURBALLS) is looking for one utterly rotten and loathsome scoundrel to join our secret lawbreaking society. Have you ever taken over the world? Led an army of crocodile robots? Thrown your enemies into a Pit of Doom? Then we want you to join us in our Fortress of Mayhem! Please write to us about your most horrible deed. Only the single most rotten and beastly scoundrel will be accepted.
Sincerely,
Mr. Maniacal, Evildoer

Zachary let loose a horrible laugh. The cackle echoed through the walls of the fort down to the ground below.

This was it. This was the way out of Good Samaritan School.

All he needed now was a diabolical scheme and maybe a henchman. All bad guys need a henchman to do things like carry their heavy laser guns, fire their Earth-melting missiles from the Moon, and clean their tree forts.

Moments later, Zachary heard a knock at the door. Strange. He didn't normally have visitors. In fact, he had never before had a visitor to his tree fort. Which is just how he liked it. "Go away."

Another knock. Zachary's grin turned into a menacing scowl. "Who is it?"

The door swung open. A plump ten-year-old boy with freckles popped his head inside. It was the same boy from outside the fish store.

"Do you have any hyenas in here?" the boy asked. "I was walking by and heard a hyena with the hiccups."

"No, that was my horrible, evil cackle." Zachary frowned. "I've been practicing, too."

"Well, keep practicing," said the boy. "We just moved in down the street. My name is Newton, but you can call me Newt."

"I'm Zachary. But you can call me Zachary," said Zachary. "Only rotten people are allowed in here, Newt." He said "Newt" with a particularly nasty snarl. "Didn't you see the sign?"

Zachary pointed to his open door. A poster board taped on it read Secret Hideout—Only Rotten People Allowed.

"I'm rotten," said Newt with a happy grin.

Zachary looked at him skeptically. "Rotten people don't have happy grins."

Newt frowned.

"Better." Zachary continued to study him. "Do you like puppies?"

"Sure."

"Everyone knows rotten people don't like puppies. You can look it up," said Zachary, dismissing Newt with a wave of his hand.

Newt blinked. "I can learn to be rotten. I don't have to like puppies."

Zachary wasn't sure someone could suddenly choose to dislike puppies. But he could use help getting into SOURBALLS.

"I need a henchman," said Zachary, thinking. "Can you clean a tree fort?"

"Sure, but I don't do windows." Newt walked inside the fort, cleared away some old tire parts and an empty can of

DR. F. FRECKLES

soup, and sat down. The fort smelled like musty, sweaty socks. The wooden floor slats creaked like bullfrogs.

Zachary shook his head. "I'm still not sure. You have lots of freckles, and rotten people don't usually have freckles. Except for Dr. Felonious Freckles, the famous mad scientist. But all his freckles are in the shape of small rats. Are yours?"

Newt looked at his arms. "Um, maybe this one?"

Zachary peered closely. The freckle looked more like a kitten than a rat. Still, he couldn't be picky if he wanted to join SOURBALLS.

His thoughts were interrupted by a

knock at the door.

"What is this? A tree fort convention?" he shouted. But before he could say anything else the door swung open. Amanda Goodbar stood in the doorway. She looked angry.

"There you are," she said. "I hope you're happy. I got in a lot of trouble because of your mustard trick. My parents are taking away my allowance for a month."

Zachary grinned. "What do you want?"

"Revenge." She held a squeeze bottle of mustard.

Zachary stood up. "You wouldn't dare use that. You don't have the guts."

"Try me." She pointed the mustard at Zachary.

"Can't we talk about this?" said Zachary, putting his hands up. "I thought you only did good, decent things."

"Battling rotten people is always good."

Amanda squinted. "Say your prayers, Ruthless."

The mustard squirted out in a loud *blurrpp!* and Zachary cringed. But just as he saw the yellow goop blob into the air, a blur of freckles flew in front of him.

Splattt!

Newt had leaped in front of Zachary, but now he tumbled to the floor, a giant circle of mustard dripping from his shirt.

As Amanda stood, stunned, Zachary bounded over and grabbed the mustard out of her hand.

"Who is that?" she gasped, pointing at Newt as he moaned on the ground.

"That's my henchman," said Zachary proudly.

Amanda stepped backward. "This isn't over, Ruthless. Not by a long shot." She ran out the door and slammed it behind her.

Newt sat up. "It's not easy being a henchman."

"Oh, stop complaining. We have bigger problems than Amanda Goodbar. We have to plan MY MOST ROTTEN CAPER EVER! Then I can join the Society of Utterly Rotten, Beastly, and Loathsome Lawbreaking Scoundrels."

Zachary shoved his copy of *Super Villain Weekly* at Newt.

"'Angry raccoons attack hotel! Hundreds flee!'" read Newt.

"No, not that! This!" said Zachary, pointing to the ad.

Newt read it and then looked up. "What's SOURBALLS?"

"SOURBALLS is only the most horrendous evil band of villains ever assembled!" cried Zachary. "They make the Band of Awful, Diabolical, 'n' Evil Wiseguy Scum (BADNEWS) look like Boy Scouts. They make the Secret Clan of Rotten, Evil, and Monstrously Infamous No Gooders (SCREAMING) look like amateurs. Being a member of SOURBALLS means you're the worst of the worst. The most rotten of the rotten. The most no good of the no good!"

Newt smiled at Zachary. "It sounds so glamorous."

Zachary sighed. "It is, but hundreds of

villains are going to answer this ad, Newt. I just have to get into SOURBALLS. Then I can live in their Fortress of Mayhem. If not . . ." Zachary continued in a whisper, "my parents will send me to Good Samaritan School." Zachary buried his face into his hands.

Newt patted him on the shoulder. "I'm sure we'll think of some terrible deed you can do. You sound like a really despicable person."

"Thank you." Zachary sniffled.

Zachary and Newt sat on the tree fort floor, staring at each other. After a

while, Newt clapped his hands together. "I know! We'll turn Lake Winnebago into cottage cheese!"

Zachary threw his arms up. "That's not evil. A lot of people like cottage cheese."

They both stared at each other some more.

"I've got it!" Zachary cried out. "I'll launch a rocket that will destroy all life on the planet."

Newt paused. "That seems a little too evil."

"I guess so. Besides, if all life was destroyed, there wouldn't be anything good to watch on TV."

Zachary picked dirt from his fingernails. Newt tapped his fingers on his knee. Then Zachary rubbed his hands together.

"Are your hands cold?" asked Newt.

"No, I'm plotting an evil plan. Rotten

people always rub their hands together when they plot evil plans."

Newt rubbed his hands together. "It's not working for me. I'm not thinking of anything evil. But my hands are warmer."

Zachary stood up, rubbed his hands faster and faster, and paced in circles until he got dizzy. Finally, he stopped. "I know! I'll turn the mayor into a zombie who will do everything I say. Then I can rule over the entire town!"

"Great idea! But how?"

"With a zombie laser, obviously," said Zachary.

"You have a zombie laser?" Newt asked.

"Not yet. We have to go where all super villains get their evil gear. On the internet at evilbadguystuff.com."

4

EVILBADGUYSTUFF.COM

Zachary led Newt down the tree fort steps, across his yard, and into his cheery lavender house with its large, inviting porch and big, bright windows. Why couldn't they live in an underground sewer or a decaying evil fortress? *Someday*, thought Zachary. *Hopefully, someday soon.*

When they entered the house, a giant

poster of a puppy stared at them from the hallway.

"I thought rotten people hated puppies," said Newt.

Zachary stomped his foot on the floor. "It's not mine!"

A voice called from the next room, "Is that you, sweetiekins?" Zachary's face turned red. Newt started to giggle until Zachary glared at him.

"I'm with my new friend Newt. We're going to my room."

"Have fun, honey bunny!"

Zachary turned to Newt. "If you repeat any of this conversation to anyone, I'll fill your ears with Cheez Whiz."

Zachary's room looked normal enough. A few posters of baseball players hung on the walls. The bedspread was dotted with little choo-choo trains. In a bookcase were books like *I Love Yarn, The Encyclopedia of Whistling,* and *The Happy Panda Bear.*

COUNT BOOGERSNOT

"I don't get it," said Newt. "This doesn't look rotten at all."

Zachary smiled, closed the door, and locked it. He turned his bedspread over to reveal a pattern of vampires and evil ghouls. The posters on the wall were on panels that flipped over to become posters of menacing criminals.

"Who are they?" asked Newt.

"Some of the most wonderfully awful villains ever," said Zachary, beaming. "The guy with the giant nose is Count Boogersnot. He can break down a bank wall with one sneeze. Next to him is Baron Burp. His belches are loud enough to shatter glass. Over there is Professor Fartalot. I bet you can figure out what he does. At the end is the worst

MR. HAPPY FACE

42

of the bunch, Mr. Happy Face, who is famous for having the worst bad guy name ever."

"I've never seen such wickedness."

Zachary sighed happily. "I know. Aren't they terrific?"

"But what about the books?"

Zachary grabbed *The History of Dandelions* and removed the jacket. The title now read *The Malevolent Musings of Mr. Maniacal.* "Never judge a book by its cover," said Zachary.

Moments later, the computer on Zachary's desk lit up with a dreary, grayish brown glow. The screen filled with pictures of evil gadgets like ray guns that

melted bank vaults, radioactive shark tanks, and hot dogs that made your teeth fall out. Everything was for sale, perfect for villains eager to rob banks, get rid of archenemies, or just cause a general nuisance at parties.

Zachary scrolled down the long list of evil products, looking past wart-growing lotions, oversize vicious sloths, beds of nails, and popcorn balls.

"What do villains do with popcorn balls?" asked Newt.

"Eat them, of course. Bad guys get hungry, too." Zachary pointed to the screen. "Look, there's a rocket to destroy all life on the planet!"

"Didn't we decide that seemed a little too evil?"

"Right, I forgot," said Zachary, nodding. He continued scanning through evil products. He halted when he reached the section labeled Lasers. "Ah—here we go."

"Cool!"

"They have lasers that freeze people. Lasers that melt people. Lasers that turn people into chipmunks, and chipmunks that turn people into lasers!" said Zachary.

"None of those seem right," said Newt.

"Look at this! 'Zombie Lasers. Turn your friends, family, and enemies into mindless zombies who eat brains and obey your every word.'"

"That sounds perfect. How much does it cost?"

"Two million dollars," Zachary grumbled.

"Being an evil mastermind sure is expensive."

"That's why bad guys always have to rob banks and stuff. Luckily, I've been saving my allowance."

Zachary took a large ceramic-tarantula jar from under his bed and dropped it on the floor. It shattered into dozens

of tiny black shards.

Zachary looked down at all the money lying among the broken pieces. "I wonder how much I have. It looks like a lot." He slowly counted the dollars and the coins. Then he counted them again.

"Well? Do you have two million dollars?" asked Newt.

"We're a little short. I have twelve dollars and thirty-six cents."

"What can you get for twelve dollars and thirty-six cents?"

Zachary shrugged. He turned back to the computer and quickly searched through pages of evil gizmos. Everything cost a lot more than $12.36. But just when Zachary was about to give up hope, an item in small type at the very bottom of the screen caught his eye.

"Here's something," Zachary said. "'Special Clearance Sale: A big Box of

Rotten. Boxes filled with all sorts of surprise evil goodies. Who knows what havoc they will bring? Every box is different.'"

"That sounds interesting. How much is it?" asked Newt.

"Twelve dollars and thirty-five cents."

"Talk about lucky—and you still have a penny left!"

"It comes with free shipping, too. I just hope this Box of Rotten is filled with really rotten things. Maybe it will have something that will turn the mayor into a zombie. Otherwise, I might never get into SOURBALLS."

MR. MANIACAL

MADAM TORTURE

DR. INDIGESTIBLE

It was getting late. Newt left, and Zachary lay down

48

on his bed with his copy of *The Malevolent Musings of Mr. Maniacal.* Inside were large color photos of the members of SOURBALLS grimacing madly with their fearsome faces: Dr. Indigestible,

G. GREEDYPUS

Gregory Greedypus, Madam Torture, Duck-Faced Floyd, the Amazing Professor Squid, and of course their leader, Mr. Maniacal, leading his Legions of Destruction.

PROF. SQUID

Zachary put the book down but then felt something under him on his bed. The Good Samaritan School brochure. His parents must have placed it there. Suddenly he was flooded with images of smiling Good Samaritan kids, petting puppies and laughing. They sang campfire songs. They hugged.

Zachary's head spun and his stomach felt queasy. He ran outside, across the yard, and up his tree fort steps. He needed the reassuring smell of sweaty socks.

5

★ ☠ ★

NO GOOD LIMA BEAN BARS

In the tree fort the next day, Zachary's hands were shaking. A small box sat on the floor.

"That was fast," said Newt. "Didn't you order this yesterday?"

"Super villains don't like to wait."

Newt leaned over closer to look. A sticker on the small box read Extra Healthy Lima Bean Bars.

"But what evil deed can you do with lima bean bars?" asked Newt.

"These aren't lima bean bars!" said Zachary, gesturing excitedly. "The post office won't deliver packages that say Box of Rotten, or Fragile—Diabolical Earth-Destroying Ray Gun Inside. So boxes from evilbadguystuff.com have labels like Happy Fuzzy Children's Books, or Goody Two-shoes Homework Helpers. The post office police don't suspect a thing."

"Wow, that's clever."

"Rotten people always are! I only hope this box is filled with fantastically rotten things. I bet lots of evil people are trying to get into SOURBALLS. We have no time to lose!"

Newt looked in the box and removed a jar of bugs. "Boll weevils. Yech."

Zachary stroked the jar. "Aren't they cute?"

Newt continued pulling things out of the box. "Here's a can of Super Strong Silly String. A pack of gum. Gum isn't rotten."

"It's zucchini-flavored gum," said Zachary. "Which is a particularly rotten flavor of gum."

Newt nodded. "Here's a large rubber cockroach. A pair of

hypno-glasses. And a T-shirt that says Born to be Rotten. How are you going to get into SOURBALLS with this junk?"

"Wait. Did you say hypno-glasses?"

"It says, 'Three-minute hypno-glasses. Hypnotize people for three minutes.'"

Zachary and Newt looked at the glasses. Then they looked at the glasses. Then they looked at the glasses. Then they looked at the glasses.

Three minutes later, Zachary blinked and said, "Wow, they work. We were both hypnotized! I can use these to turn the mayor into a zombie and take over the town!"

"Great idea! But you only have three minutes. That's not a lot of time."

Zachary nodded. "I'll have to write a list of all the marvelously rotten things I can make the mayor do in three minutes." He took an old cell phone from his pocket. "I'm only supposed to use this for urgent phone calls," said Zachary. "But what could be more urgent than getting into SOURBALLS?"

Zachary dialed the mayor's office. Mayor Mudfogg's personal assistant, Mrs. Boozle, answered the phone.

"Yes, we'd like to see him as soon as possible," said Zachary. After a moment he turned to Newt and whispered, "She wants to know why we need to see the mayor."

"To turn him into a zombie and take over the town," said Newt.

Zachary rolled his eyes. "I can't say that! She'll never let us see the mayor."

"Good point," said Newt.

Zachary stared at the Box of Rotten and then smiled. That might work. "We're selling Extra Healthy Lima Bean Bars," he said.

"Oh, good! Mayor Mudfogg loves lima bean bars," said Mrs. Boozle. "I'm glad they're extra healthy, too. Last week I bought the mayor lima bean bars that were only sort of healthy. These sound much better." She paused. "You're telling the truth, right? You don't really want to turn the mayor into a zombie and take over the town, do you?"

"Who, us?" stammered Zachary. He

NO RUNNING

blinked, and then remembered he was on the phone and she couldn't see him. "Why would you think that?"

"You can never be too careful. But I think I hear you blinking, so you can't be up to anything too rotten. The mayor can see you tomorrow at eleven A.M."

"That was close," Zachary said to Newt as he hung up the phone. "What diabolical things should we have him do? Put barracudas in the swimming pools? Outlaw smiles? Destroy all life on the planet?" Newt looked at Zachary and shook his head. Zachary sighed. "Right.

That last one is too evil."

"I know!" said Newt. "We can have him quack like a duck. I saw a hypnotist do that on TV once. It was real funny."

Zachary sneered. "That's not evil."

"Quacking like a duck could be evil, if it's an evil duck."

"We only have three minutes—we can't waste it on ducks. Now leave me alone. I have rotten plans to form!" said Zachary, who immediately began rubbing his hands and laughing.

"Sorry, but your cackle still sounds like a hyena with the hiccups," said Newt.

"Really? I practiced last night right before bedtime, too," Zachary grumbled.

As Newt left the tree fort, Zachary paced the creaky tree fort floor, imagining the SOURBALLS team flying him away in their evil blimp toward the Fortress of Mayhem.

6

MAYOR MUDFOGG

The next morning, Zachary and Newt walked briskly across town. As the henchman, it was Newt's job to carry the box.

"Remember, let me do all the talking," said Zachary.

On the sidewalk next to them a large bush rustled. "What's that?"

"Just a large, rustling bush," Newt said.

"I thought I saw someone." Zachary squinted. Nope, just a bush. "I must be nervous about our plan. Look, we're here."

They stood across the street from Capitol Hall, the enormous office mansion of Mayor Mudfogg. It had tall pillars out front and a large, majestic dome so high Zachary had to crane his neck to see the top. A flag flapped from the roof. Zachary thought it looked almost as impressive as a secret, sprawling, evil castle. Almost.

They walked closer, approaching the tall steel fence surrounding the building. Two burly armed guards stood in front of the gate. One of the guards had a large bushy red beard. The other had

a large bushy red mustache.

"Hi, we're here to see the mayor," said Zachary.

The bushy-red-bearded guard looked down and studied them carefully. "We're not supposed to let in rotten people. Are you rotten?"

"Who, us?" said Zachary, blinking.

"Well, you are blinking a lot," said the bushy-red-mustached guard. He looked at them carefully. "Rotten people wear shirts that say things like Born to be Rotten. Are you wearing one?"

"Of course not," said Zachary, glad he had left his new shirt in the box.

"Then I guess you can go in," said the mustached guard.

Newt held tightly to the Box of Rotten as they walked past the guards and up the long marble steps into the building.

They stood in a cavernous rotunda that tapered into a shining golden dome roof. The floors were marble and the walls gleamed like polished silver.

"This place is awesome," whispered Newt.

"Why are you whispering?" Zachary whispered back.

Newt shrugged. "I bet being the mayor is the coolest job in the world."

"Not as cool as being in SOURBALLS, or being a villain whose job it is to turn a mayor into a zombie," Zachary said.

Newt nodded and then pointed to a hallway with a series of doors. "Over here." The very first door had a sign that read Mayor Mudfogg's Office. Zachary took a deep breath and walked in. Newt followed him closely.

The first thing they saw was a life-size statue of Mayor Mudfogg. His arms were open wide, greeting everyone who entered. He smiled warmly. He looked like someone's favorite uncle.

"He looks nice," said Newt.

"If you like that sort of thing," Zachary grumbled.

Mrs. Boozle, the mayor's personal assistant, sat behind a desk, talking to a

tall man who did not look like anyone's
uncle, unless it was someone's rotten
uncle who no one spoke to anymore. He
had a long pointy nose; eyebrows that
slanted downward in a foul-looking way;
and a mouthful of black, gnarly teeth.

"I'm sorry, Mr. Snodgrass," said Mrs.
Boozle. "The mayor is booked right now.
Then we will both be out at a meeting
until one."

"But I have important business," said Mr. Snodgrass.

"I don't like the look of this guy," whispered Newt. "It looks like he's up to something."

"I know," Zachary said with a dreamy smile. "He seems wonderfully evil."

"I'm sorry, Mr. Snodgrass," said Mrs. Boozle. "Can we expect you at one?"

"Fine. But I'm not happy about it." Mr. Snodgrass stomped past the boys, sneered at the statue of Mayor Mudfogg, and stormed out the door.

Zachary and Newt approached Mrs. Boozle. She peered up from underneath her large mop of curly white hair. "Who was that?" asked Zachary.

"That's the lieutenant mayor, Snicker Snodgrass," said Mrs. Boozle. "He works in the office next door." She leaned over confidentially. "Does he look like he's up to something?"

Zachary shrugged.

"Anyway, what can I do for you boys?" she asked.

"I'm Zachary and this is Newt. We have an appointment with Mayor Mudfogg."

"Oh, yes. Here it is," she said as she checked her computer log. "You're here to sell Extra Healthy Lima Bean Bars. They are the mayor's favorite! Please have a seat and he'll be with you in a moment." She gestured to some chairs against the wall, and Zachary and Newt sat down.

"Remember," Zachary whispered to Newt, "the hypno-glasses will only hypnotize Mayor Mudfogg for three minutes."

"I just want him to quack like a duck," said Newt.

Zachary stared daggers. "We're not here to have fun. We're here to do rotten things so I'll get into SOURBALLS. Look at My Marvelous List of Rotten! I worked all night on it." He handed Newt a piece of paper.

Newt handed the Marvelous List of Rotten back to Zachary. "Those are all very rotten things."

"I know," agreed Zachary. "But we only have three minutes, so we need to act fast."

Mrs. Boozle smiled at them. "You can go in now."

She opened the heavy wooden door leading into Mayor Mudfogg's room, and Zachary and Newt entered. The office seemed to stretch on and on and up and up. They walked past a suit of armor with an ax, pictures of the mayor shaking hands with sport stars and celebrities, and a mysterious object covered by a black cloth that reached all the way to the ceiling. At the end of the room, Mayor Mudfogg sat behind a desk, rubbing his hands together. When he saw Zachary and Newt, he stood up and smiled.

"Welcome, I'm Mayor Mudfogg!" he said in a booming voice. "You must be Zachary and Newt."

Zachary pointed to the mysterious cloth-covered object they walked past. "What's that?"

"That is a, um, a secret gift to the city." The mayor coughed. "It will make quite a splash, I promise you."

"Can we see it?" asked Newt.

"No!" said Mudfogg with alarm. "I mean, it's a surprise. We wouldn't want to spoil it, would we? But you'll see it soon. Everyone will." He smiled. "Are you boys here selling Extra Healthy Lima Bean Bars?"

"That's right," said Zachary, grabbing the box from Newt. As he held it up to show Mayor Mudfogg, Zachary swallowed an evil cackle.

"I'll be honest," said the mayor. "I hate lima bean bars. Mrs. Boozle keeps on buying them for me, but they make me sick. Oh, well. She's new, and it's hard to get good help." He reached out his hand. "But I suppose I can buy one lima bean bar

since you've come all this way. At least
they are extra healthy."

Zachary opened the box. But instead
of a lima bean bar he took out a pair of
hypno-glasses, which he quickly slipped
over his eyes. The mayor looked into
Zachary's glasses. His jaw dropped open
and his eyes stared blankly.

7

★ 💀 ★

MONKEYING AROUND

"You will obey every word," said Zachary.

"I . . . will . . . obey . . . every . . . word," Mudfogg repeated.

"This is great." Newt giggled. "Now, quack like a duck!"

"Quack, quack!"

Zachary shook his fist. "Stop monkeying around! We only have three minutes.

We have to get through My Marvelous List of Rotten."

"Just one more time, please?" said Newt. "Quack again!"

"Quack, quack!"

"I said, stop monkeying around," snapped Zachary.

"I am not," protested Newt.

"You *are* monkeying around!" Zachary thumped his foot on the floor.

"Eeep!" said Mayor Mudfogg, scratching his head. "Ooh, ooh, ooh!" He jumped on his desk

and started swinging his arms back and forth.

"What's he doing?" asked Newt. "He's acting like an ape."

Zachary slapped his hand on his forehead. "No, he's acting like a monkey. He's monkeying around! Look what you've done!"

"All I told him to do was quack. You're the one who told him to be a monkey," said Newt.

While they argued, Mayor Mudfogg leaped from his desk and grabbed the light fixture on the ceiling. He swung back and forth.

"If anyone sees him like this, they'll throw him in the loony bin," said Zachary.

Mudfogg swung faster, the light shook, and tiny paint crumbs began raining down from all around it. Zachary thought the whole fixture might crash to the ground. "Quick, help me catch him!"

But Mayor Mudfogg was as fast as a monkey, too. When Zachary reached for him, the mayor swung off the light and headed toward the door, half jumping and half skipping.

"Eeep! Ooh, ooh, ooh!" Mudfogg hollered.

"If he makes it out the door, I'll never get through My Marvelous List of Rotten!" yelled Zachary, tossing his glasses on the desk and running behind the leaping monkey mayor. "Stop!"

Mudfogg stopped. Unfortunately,

Zachary didn't.

Zachary stumbled over the mayor, unable to slow himself, and flew straight at the suit of armor. He smashed into it with a loud, horrifying crash. Heavy steel parts clanked to the ground, and the armored ax swung down with a rusty screech, narrowly missing Zachary's head.

"Help!" yelled Zachary. "Help!"

The door swung open and Mrs. Boozle

ran in. "What happened? Is everyone okay?"

Zachary kept his head down and his hands covering his eyes.

"Oh, my," said a concerned Mayor Mudfogg. He no longer sounded like a monkey. "What happened? I can't remember anything from the last three minutes, although I do have a strong desire to eat a banana."

Mayor Mudfogg helped Zachary to his feet.

"My boy, I have no idea how you crashed into my armor," the mayor said. "Please have a seat while I stick my head out the window to get some air. For some reason, I feel all jumpy." As Mayor Mudfogg walked to his window, Mrs. Boozle exited the room.

Meanwhile, Newt stood at the mayor's desk, reading a piece of paper and looking very concerned. He waved Zachary over frantically. "We need to get out of here," he whispered.

"But I still need to go through My Marvelous List of Rotten," insisted Zachary.

"While you were busy attacking that suit of armor, I found this on the mayor's desk." Newt handed Zachary the paper.

FROM THE DESK OF MAYOR MUDFOGG

Dear Evil Sirs,
I am writing in hopes of joining the Society of Utterly Rotten, Beastly, and Loathsome Lawbreaking Scoundrels (SOURBALLS). As mayor, I have been planning rotten schemes to cement my place in the halls of villainy. Just recently, I purchased a laser that will turn everyone in town into zombies who eat brains and do everything I say. Now, what could be more evil?

Evilly Yours,
Mayor Maynard P. Mudfogg

"Hey, that was my idea!" growled Zachary. "He must have bought the laser from evilbadguystuff.com. We'll have to stop him."

"So we can save the town?" asked Newt.

"No! If he turns everyone in town into zombies, he'll get into SOURBALLS and not me!" said Zachary.

"What should we do?"

"Good question." Zachary rubbed his

hands together. "We'll have to hypnotize him again until I can think of something."

"Now why would I let you do that?" said Mayor Mudfogg. Zachary turned around to see the mayor standing right behind them.

"Oh, no! Quick—put on your glasses," shouted Newt.

"Where are they?" Zachary scanned the desk frantically.

"Looking for these?" Mayor Mudfogg held the glasses in his hand and crushed them with his fist. He let loose an evil laugh. "Bwa-ha-ha."

"Wow, that's a really good laugh," said Zachary. "All

my evil laughs sound like a hyena with the hiccups."

"Thanks, I've been practicing. But now I need to begin my diabolical scheme."

"You won't get away with it, Mudfogg," said Newt, hands on his hips. "We'll tell everyone your secret plan."

"Who's going to believe a couple of kids like you?" Mayor Mudfogg cackled again. "Bwa-ha-ha!" Zachary listened enviously.

The door behind them opened, and the two burly redheaded guards from outside the gate walked into the room.

"I doubt anyone would believe you," said Mudfogg, "but I can't take the chance." Mayor Mudfogg pointed to Zachary and Newt and shouted to the guards, "Lock these two rotten kids up!"

"We're not rotten, he is!" Newt pointed to the mayor.

"Actually, we're rotten, too," said Zachary.

The guards approached them, angry eyes glaring.

"Quick! Run!" yelled Zachary.

Newt was too slow. The bushy-red-bearded guard grabbed him, pinning his arms behind his back. "Hey, that hurts," Newt whined.

The bushy-red-mustached guard reached for Zachary, but Zachary poked him in the eye.

"Hey, that was a rotten thing to do!" cried the guard.

Zachary flushed with pride as he ran over to the pile of armor still strewn about the floor. "Take this!" Zachary yelled, throwing an armored helmet at

the mustached guard.
The guard blocked it with his arm.

"Let's not *lose our heads*," said Mudfogg.

Zachary groaned. Lots of bad guys love telling bad puns when battling enemies, but few are really good at it.

Mudfogg wasn't.

Zachary picked up an armored glove, and then threw it at the guard.

"It looks like you're *empty-handed*," Mudfogg yelled.

Zachary rolled his eyes and threw an armored elbow, an armored chest, belly, back, arm, thigh, hip, and foot.

"You've got no *body* left," snarled Mudfogg. "Get him!"

The guard rushed toward Zachary, who bounded over to the armored ax still wedged into the floor.

"Don't move!" Zachary yelled. "I have this ax, see? And I'm going out that door. You're not going to try to stop me, either. I am Zachary Ruthless! I am cunning, rotten, and dangerous!!" and then he laughed wickedly.

"Great speech, Zachary!" Newt hooted.

"Yes, but your laugh sounds like a

hyena with the hiccups," said Mudfogg. "And that ax weighs three hundred pounds. You'll never be able to move it."

"Oh." Zachary frowned, unsure if he was more upset over his lousy laugh or the extra heavy ax. The mustached guard grabbed Zachary's arm.

Zachary looked at him and blinked.

"But he's blinking," complained the guard. "He looks so innocent!"

"Then don't look at him, you fool! Tie these rotten kids up and get them out of here!" demanded Mudfogg. "I'll deal with them later."

As Zachary was dragged away, he caught a glimpse outside the window. He thought he saw a shadow watching them. But then he looked again, and the shadow was gone.

8

BATTLING BOLL WEEVILS

Zachary and Newt were led to an empty office down the hall. Their hands were bound behind their backs with rope. Their feet were tied, too. Other than being able to slowly wiggle on their butts, the boys were helpless.

"You can wiggle on your butts as much as you like," said the bearded guard, "but you won't be able to get out of here."

"Just to make sure, we'll be waiting

right outside!" said the mustached guard. "But don't try any tricks to get us to open this door. Because we won't fall for any!"

"What should we do with this box of lima bean bars?" The bearded guard held the Box of Rotten. "I love lima bean bars."

The mustached guard looked back at Zachary and Newt. "I love them, too. But give the box back to these rotten kids. They might be in here for a while."

They laughed, tossed the box to Zachary and Newt, and then slammed the door behind them.

"I can't believe Mayor Mudfogg is evil," said Newt. "He seemed so nice. Not like that Snodgrass guy."

"You can't judge a book by its cover," said Zachary. "But we still have our Box of Rotten."

"So what?" said Newt. "It's filled with junk."

Zachary thought about all the things in the box. A jar of boll weevils, a can of Super Strong Silly String, a pack of zucchini-flavored gum, a large rubber cockroach, and a T-shirt that said Born to be Rotten. He also had a penny in his pocket.

He needed to hatch a plan. Although his hands were tied, he was still able to rub them. Suddenly, Zachary's mouth curved into a big grin. "Of course! We have a jar of boll weevils!"

"So?" asked Newt.

"Boll weevils eat cotton!"

"You want them to eat your shirt?" asked Newt.

"This rope is made out of cotton. If I can open the jar, maybe the boll weevils will eat through my rope! Then we can escape and find the zombie laser."

Zachary wiggled on his butt until his back faced the Box of Rotten. He groped until he snapped it open, then he felt for the glass jar. Holding it steady with one

hand, Zachary slowly untwisted the lid with the other.

"I'm getting it!" Zachary shouted. "It's twisting, twisting . . ."

Seconds later, Newt heard the clank of the jar lid falling, followed by Zachary giggling.

"This isn't a time to laugh."

"Sorry! But the boll weevils are crawling on my wrists and it tickles!" said Zachary.

But they both knew the boll weevils weren't just crawling on Zachary's wrists. They were feasting on the delicate cotton fibers of the rope, chewing and weakening the cords.

"I can feel them getting looser," said Zachary. "I can feel the rope starting to shred! I can feel them tickling me!"

"C'mon, guys! Just a few more bites!"

encouraged Newt. Then, suddenly, Zachary's hands were free. He untied the ropes around his feet, and Newt's ropes, too.

"We still have to get past the guards," said Zachary. "We need a plan."

"If only we can get the guards to open the door," said Newt. "Then we can rush past them and call the police."

Zachary put his hands on his hips. "Rotten people who want to join SOURBALLS don't call the police."

"Right. Sorry. But we still need to get the guards to open the door."

"But how?"

"I know!" said Newt. "We'll scream we're being attacked by angry squirrels."

Zachary threw his hands up. "Angry squirrels? That makes no sense!" Then Zachary smiled. "I know! We'll say we're being attacked by angry raccoons."

"That's much better," agreed Newt.

Zachary took a deep breath, and then screamed as loudly as he could, "HELP! ANGRY RACCOONS!" Newt joined in the yelling.

The door swung open and the two guards rushed inside. "Are angry raccoons in here?" the bearded guard asked.

"Wh-where are they?" asked the mustached guard. He trembled and then glared at Newt's free arms. "Hey, wait! They're loose! It's a trick!"

"I don't know how you got those ropes untied," said the bearded guard. "It's not like we have boll weevils running around. Now we'll have to teach you a lesson."

Zachary took a step back. He needed to distract them. He opened his Box of Rotten and grabbed the large rubber cockroach, tossing it under one of the guards' feet.

"Look! It's an angry raccoon!" yelled Zachary.

The bearded guard jumped, and then landed on the slippery rubber cockroach. His feet flew up in the air. The mustached guard couldn't get out of the way. Their heads collided with a loud *thud!* Both guards crumpled to the ground.

"What luck! They're both knocked out cold," said Newt. "Now let's get out of here."

"Not until we find that laser," said Zachary.

"So you can destroy it and save the town?"

"No, so I can turn Mudfogg into a zombie, go over My Marvelous List of Rotten, and get into SOURBALLS. Saving the town is kind of against the whole point of this."

"But we'll never find it," said Newt. "This place is huge. The laser could be anywhere."

Zachary handed Newt the Box of Rotten and rubbed his hands together. "If I had a zombie laser, I would keep it close by me so I could do evil at a moment's notice. I'd hide it in a closet or maybe my office."

"But we didn't see a laser hiding in his office," said Newt.

"Of course not!" Zachary snapped his

fingers. "It was covered up! Mudfogg said that black cloth was hiding a surprise. The surprise is the laser!"

"You're right! But how can we get past Mudfogg?" asked Newt.

"Mrs. Boozle told Snodgrass she and Mayor Mudfogg would be in a meeting until one." Zachary pointed at a clock on the wall. "It's only twelve forty-five. The office will be empty for another fifteen minutes!"

They exited the room and locked the door behind them in case the guards woke up. Then they rushed over to the mayor's office across the hall.

It was empty. Zachary's heart beat madly. SOURBALLS was so close he could taste it.

9

ZOMBIES

Zachary and Newt stood next to the large object covered by the black cloth. It stood twice the height of Zachary and Newt, if Zachary stood on Newt's head. Zachary took a deep breath, grabbed the cloth, and pulled.

It was everything an evil bad guy laser should be. Red and green lights blinked across its metallic frame. A large crane emerged from the top.

"That's the zombie laser. I recognize it from the website," said Newt.

"Let's figure out how to use it, so we can zap Mudfogg when he comes back from his meeting," said Zachary. "SOURBALLS, here I come!"

"It looks like I underestimated you boys."

Zachary and Newt turned to see Mayor Mudfogg enter the office. He closed the door behind him.

"It's a good thing my meeting ended early, or you boys might have gotten away with your plan. I don't know how you got past my guards, but I guess I'll have to take care of you once and for all." The mayor's mouth twisted into an evil grin. "You'll be my very first zombies! Bwa-ha-ha-ha!"

Zachary listened fondly to the laugh.

Newt nudged him. "Focus!"

Mudfogg walked toward them.

"What can we do?" asked Newt, backing up.

"What do we have left in the Box of Rotten?" asked Zachary.

Newt opened the box. "We've got some Super Strong Silly String."

"Perfect!" said Zachary. "Toss it over."

"I can handle this!" said Newt, holding up the can.

"Henchmen don't handle secret weapons. Give it to me!"

"There's no time!" Mudfogg was only steps away. Newt aimed the can, pushed the button, and released a torrent of string in the air.

Unfortunately, Newt held the canister backward. Super Strong Silly String covered Zachary's and Newt's faces, eyes, hands, and bodies.

"I can't see!" screamed Zachary.

"I can't move!" screamed Newt.

The string stuck on them like glue, binding their arms.

"That's why henchmen never handle secret weapons!" yelled Zachary. "Look what you've done!"

"Oops," Newt said. "Sorry."

"Bwa-ha-ha!" laughed Mudfogg.

Zachary managed to free one of his hands and clawed at the string wrapped

around his eyes. He now saw the zombie laser pointed directly down at them. Mayor Mudfogg stood behind the machine.

"Just stand still for a moment, boys. You won't feel a thing," said Mudfogg as he fiddled with the controls.

"Run!" shrieked Newt, removing string

from his eyes, too.

"This Super Strong Silly String is everywhere! I can't move my legs."

Zachary opened the Box of Rotten with his free hand.

"Is there anything in there that can save us?" asked Newt.

Meanwhile, the zombie laser began to rumble.

"I've still got some zucchini-flavored gum," said Zachary. "That could work!"

"This is no time to chew gum!" yelled Newt.

Zachary popped the gum into his mouth.

Now the zombie laser glowed red.

"Ew, this tastes exactly like zucchini!" Zachary shot the gum out of his mouth. It flew three feet up in the air and landed directly on the tip of the laser lens. It stuck with a soft *splat*!

"Good-bye, boys," said Mudfogg. "Prepare to be zombie-fried!" The tip of the laser flashed a bright light. The machine let loose a loud *wckzzrr* and then a giant puff of smoke gushed out the back, covering Mayor Mudfogg. The machine erupted in fiery sparks.

"What happened?" asked Newt. "I don't feel like a zombie."

"The awful zucchini flavor of the gum plugged up the laser, and it backfired into Mayor Mudfogg just like I planned."

"Then we're not zombies," said Newt.

"No, but what happened to Mayor Mudfogg?"

The mayor slowly stepped away from the laser. His face was an eerie grayish green and twisted into a misshapen sneer. His eyes bulged out and he smelled

like day-old tuna fish.

"He's turned himself into a zombie!" cried Zachary.

"Will he suck out our brains?" Newt staggered back.

"Maybe," said Zachary. "But more important, we've done it! The mayor is a zombie, just like I wanted! Now we can go through My Marvelous List of Rotten, and I'll be a member of SOURBALLS in no time!"

"Grrmmph," Mayor Mudfogg replied.

10

TUNA FISH

Just as Zachary was unfolding his Marvelous List of Rotten, someone knocked at the door.

"Go away," yelled Zachary.

"Not a chance! We have a meeting and I'm not leaving!" snapped an angry voice.

"It must be Snodgrass," said Zachary to Newt. "Quick, we have to hide. No one can see us here."

A minute later, the black cloth once

again covered the laser and the zombie mayor sat limply on his chair. Zachary and Newt crouched under his desk, huddled together in a tight lump. The smell of tuna fish filled the air. Newt and Zachary had to plug their noses to keep from getting sick.

"What's with the smell?" whispered Newt.

"All zombies smell like tuna fish. Didn't you know that?"

"How would I know that?" asked Newt.

Zachary shrugged. "I thought everyone did."

Snodgrass knocked at the door again. Zachary yelled from under the desk, "Come in!"

They heard the door open and plodding steps approach the desk.

"Mudfogg, you look awfully grayish green." Snodgrass sniffed. "And your whole room smells like tuna fish."

"I ate some lima bean bars and they

always give me gas," said Zachary, disguising his voice.

"Well, open a window or something!" Snodgrass said. "And why isn't your mouth moving when you talk?"

Zachary hesitated. "I'm practicing ventriloquism."

Zachary expected Snodgrass to leap behind the desk and find them. But instead Snodgrass said, "It's always good to learn ventriloquism. You never know when you'll have to perform in a talent show."

"What do you want?" asked Zachary. He needed Snodgrass to leave so he could begin his evil plans.

"The same things I've been warning you about for weeks. We're in a crisis! Mustard balloons are exploding. Angry raccoons are running amok. Someone might melt the capitol with a giant microwave oven!"

"But where would they find a micro-wave oven big enough?" asked Zachary.

"How do I know? That's not the point!

Drastic measures are needed! I need you to declare me ruler of the town so I'll have the power I've always dreamed of—uh, I mean, so everyone is safe from bad things," Snodgrass said.

Zachary looked at Newt, who whispered, "Tell him you'll take it under advisement. Mayors always say stuff like that."

"I'll take it under advisement," said Zachary.

Snodgrass harrumphed. "Harrumph," he said. "That's what you always say. But you'll be sorry you didn't listen to me. Everyone will be sorry."

Newt and Zachary heard something fall lightly on the floor, a door slam, and then footsteps down the hall.

Newt and Zachary came up coughing and smelling like tuna fish. "That Snodgrass is up to no good," said Newt.

"I know," said Zachary. "Isn't he terrific?"

Newt spotted a piece of paper on the

floor. "I think Snodgrass dropped that note."

"You're wasting time," said Zachary. "We need to begin going through my evil plans before we're interrupted again."

Newt picked up the piece of paper and gulped. "Listen to this," he said.

Dear SOURBALLS,
I want to join your dark, terrible society so I can finally have the power I deserve. I will ask Mayor Mudfogg to grant me total control of the town. If he refuses, I will show him! I have acquired a rocket that will destroy all life on Earth. I have secretly planted the rocket in my office where no one can find it. Everyone will be sorry they messed with me! Ha-ha-ha!

Yours rottenly,
Lt. Mayor Snicker J. Snodgrass

"If he destroys all life on the planet, all my favorite TV shows will be canceled," cried Zachary.

"Plus, we'll be goners," Newt pointed out. "His plan is a little too evil."

"I agree. We'll need to go to Snod- grass's office and find the machine."

"What about Mayor Mudfogg?" asked Newt. The mayor was still in his chair, drooling.

"I'll order him to take a nap. At least then he can't get into any trouble."

Newt crossed his fingers. "I just hope it's not too late."

HAPPY FUZZY ROCKETS

Zachary and Newt opened the office door a crack and peeked into the waiting room. No one was there.

"Mrs. Boozle isn't back yet, and those guards must still be locked up," said Newt.

Snodgrass's office was right next door. Newt and Zachary crept quietly to it, checked inside, and turned on the lights. The room was empty with only a desk, a large bookshelf, and a fern. A skylight covered the high ceiling.

"I don't see the rocket," said Newt, confused.

"Maybe there's a secret room," suggested Zachary. "Lots of bad guys have secret rooms or hidden subbasements or mysterious attics. You check the bookshelf, I'll look at the desk."

Newt moved books off and on the bookshelf. Zachary searched the desk for buttons inside and underneath and everywhere bad guys hide secret desk buttons.

"Drat! There's always a secret button," said Zachary.

"I don't see anything in the books either," said Newt.

"Wait!" said Zachary. "Do you still have Snodgrass's letter?"

"Sure." Newt handed it to Zachary, who read it carefully.

"Of course! Bad guys always leave clues. It's right here, see?"

Newt read the note. "'I have acquired a rocket that will destroy all life on Earth.'"

"Not that part. This one:

life on Earth. I have **secretly planted the rocket** in my office where no one can find it. Everyone will be sorry they

It's the plant! The only thing we didn't check was the fern!"

Zachary dashed over to the potted plant. Peering closely, he noticed a fake, plastic leaf near the bottom. Zachary tugged it. Suddenly, the floor fell away.

The sound of creaking chains filled the room as a new floor rose from the depths far below. On it was a gigantic steel rocket, gleaming with a deadly,

dull shine. The rocket pointed up, supported by a large metal brace.

On the side of the rocket a giant label read Happy Fuzzy Children's Books.

"We better destroy it," said Zachary, "although it seems like a shame to waste such a perfectly good evil machine."

"I couldn't agree more," said a voice behind them. Snodgrass entered the room and then locked the door. He held a coil of wire.

"You're just in time to watch," said Snodgrass. "When this rocket is launched, all life on this planet will be destroyed! Everyone will be sorry they didn't listen to Snicker Snodgrass!" His lips curved into a demented sneer and he let loose a bloodcurdling high-pitched laugh, "Hee, hee, hee!"

126

"Wow, that's a good laugh, too," said Zachary.

"Thanks, I've been practicing. But first, I need to take care of you two kids."

Snodgrass was surprisingly quick, and he pounced on Newt and Zachary before they could run away. He was surprisingly strong, too. Despite all their wiggling and pushing, Snodgrass wrapped the wire around them.

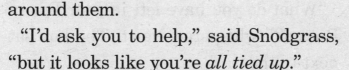

"I'd ask you to help," said Snodgrass, "but it looks like you're *all tied up*."

Zachary groaned. More terrible evildoer puns. He struggled to break the wire coil, but it was too tight. They could barely move.

"Rats, *coiled* again!" said Snodgrass. Zachary rolled his eyes.

"Too bad the *wire alarm* didn't go off!" Zachary looked at him blankly.

"Get it? Wire alarm? Fire alarm?"

"Will you stop with the puns and light the fuse already?" said Zachary.

"Fine. In a few moments the rocket will destroy everyone!" Snodgrass took a lighter out of his pocket and lit a long fuse on the bottom of the rocket. It sparked. Then he walked around to the side of the rocket and pulled a lever. Red lights began to flash all around the rocket.

"What do you have left in your Box of Rotten?" whispered Newt. The box sat next to them.

"Just the T-shirt that says Born to be Rotten," Zachary moaned.

"Do you have any more boll weevils?" Newt asked.

"No! But even if I did, boll weevils can't eat through wire," said Zachary.

"I know. I just wanted them to tickle me so I would die with a smile on my face."

The spark quickly traveled up the fuse.

"Good-bye, boys," said Snodgrass. "I'd love to stay, but I need to make my escape so I can fly off to join SOURBALLS in their evil blimp!"

With a final "hee, hee, hee!" Snodgrass ran from the room. Newt and Zachary stared at the shrinking fuse in horror.

"What do we do now? We've got to stop that rocket!" said Newt.

"We need a miracle," said Zachary.

They heard movement at the doorway and turned their heads, expecting to see Snodgrass rushing back. Instead, Amanda Goodbar walked toward them,

dressed in black. She smiled and lifted a squeeze bottle of yellow mustard in her hand. "Now I've got you."

"I knew someone was spying on us," said Zachary. "It was you!"

"Of course. And now that you're tied

up I can finally get my revenge." She walked closer and pointed the bottle at them.

"You need to stop that rocket," yelled Zachary. "It's going to destroy all life on Earth!" He pointed to the fuse that was dwindling quickly.

"I'm not going to fall for your tricks," she said.

"It's no trick!" said Newt. "Why else would we be tied up in a wire coil next to a giant rocket?"

"How do I know? I have no idea how your twisted brains work."

The wire coils were just loose enough for Zachary to plunge his hand into his pocket, searching for something that could help him.

The penny. It was still there.

He gripped it tightly in his palm.

Amanda came closer and aimed the jar

right at Zachary. "Revenge, thy name is mustard."

Zachary flipped the coin toward Amanda. His aim had to be perfect.

Just as she squirted, the coin smacked her in the eye. Amanda's arm shot up, and a blob of yellow goop plopped high in the air. Too high.

"Duck!" yelled Zachary.

"An evil hypnotized duck?" asked Newt.

"No! Incoming mustard!"

The oozing, slurpy condiment swooped toward them. Zachary felt a lone drop splash in his hair, but the rest of it shot over his head.

The fuse gave one final flare.

Then, it was covered in mustard, the yellow glop landing on the spark and smothering it.

The flame went out.

Before Zachary could take a breath of relief, the door burst open and seven police officers in armored gear rushed in, weapons at the ready and shield guards around their heads. One of the officers rushed to Zachary and Newt

and snipped off the wire with a pair of scissors. The officer removed her helmet, revealing a lock of curly white hair and giant glasses.

"Mrs. Boozle?" said Newt.

"Officer Boozle, actually," she said. "I've been undercover. We knew Snodgrass was up to no good. But we didn't know about Mudfogg. I guess you can't judge a book by its cover. I've been keeping an eye on things, watching the mail for lasers and rockets, but the only boxes that came were labeled Happy Fuzzy Children's Books. I'm not sure how they smuggled those weapons in, but it looks like you boys saved the city."

"Thanks!" said Newt with a big smile.

"Please don't use the word 'saved,'" mumbled Zachary, but Officer Boozle didn't hear him.

"Let go of me!" shouted Amanda. "I didn't do anything."

An officer was holding her arm. "We found this one armed with mustard."

Officer Boozle stared at her. "Better take her in for questioning. She looks suspicious."

"But it was my mustard that put out

the rocket!" Amanda shouted.

"You're just making things worse," said Mrs. Boozle as Amanda was dragged away.

"Did you catch Snodgrass?" asked Newt.

"Not yet, but don't worry, he can't go far. We'll get him. You boys will get a big medal for this. You're heroes."

Newt beamed.

Zachary looked as greenish gray as a zombie. As Officer Boozle walked away

Zachary said, "A medal? I guess I can forget about SOURBALLS."

"You've got plenty of time to perform terrible no-good deeds in the future," said Newt. "You're too despicable not to get in, eventually."

"You think so?" said Zachary. "Thanks!"

Newt walked over to the Box of Rotten and removed the Born to be Rotten T-shirt. "Can I have this?"

Zachary shrugged. "I guess so."

"That's nice of you," said Newt, smiling. You know, it's practically a good deed."

Zachary looked horrified for a moment, and then he grinned. "Well, just don't tell anyone."

As they walked outside, they saw Mayor Mudfogg being carried out of the building by police officers. He was still napping.

"What are you going to do about Good Samaritan School?" asked Newt.

"I suppose there's nothing I can do. But who knows? Maybe I can perform plenty of mischief there. After all, who would expect someone as rotten as me in Good Samaritan School?"

As Zachary and Newt strolled out of Capitol Hall, Zachary gave a quiet, yet evil chuckle.

Newt looked at Zachary. "Hey, that chuckle wasn't bad," said Newt. "I think you're getting the hang of it."

"Thanks, buddy," said Zachary as he momentarily felt a warm, happy feeling. Then he shuddered in disgust. He quickly wiped the thoughts from his mind and tried to concentrate on fiery death balls, giant microwave ovens, and other evil schemes as they began the long walk back to the tree fort.

SO YOU THOUGHT THE ROTTENNESS WAS OVER? THINK AGAIN!

~~DON'T~~ READ THIS ROTTEN EXCERPT FROM:

THE ROTTEN ADVENTURES OF Zachary Ruthless

THE STENCH OF GOODNESS

ALLAN WOODROW

Illustrations by AARON BLECHA

1

★ ☠ ★

1,000 CRICKETS

It took Zachary and Newt the entire week to collect 1,000 crickets. Every night they looked under rocks, by the pond, and in the woods. They had to get female crickets. That was important to the plan.

Zachary kept the crickets up all night, storing them in a shoe box next to a loud radio and below a shining flashlight. Just to be sure, Zachary occasionally walked

over to them and screamed, "Wake up, crickets!" They had to be 1,000 tired female crickets.

That was also important to the plan.

But today was the big day. Families lined the street, packed tight, waiting for the start of the annual Plentyville Fourth of July parade. An evil cackle blasted from Zachary's lips.

Newt turned to Zachary, shaking his head. "Your laugh sounds like a chicken being tickled."

"Really?" asked Zachary, frowning.

"I've been working on it, too."

Newt patted Zachary's shoulder. "Your cackle's getting better. Really! Keep practicing!" Newt slurped his giant Super Guzzle orange soda. It was his third one that morning. Newt's left eye twitched and he couldn't stop shaking his knees.

"How big is that thing?" asked Zachary.

"One hundred twenty-eight ounces of carbonated sugar!" said Newt proudly, and then burped.

Zachary shook his head. Evildoers needed to be ready to flee at a moment's notice, and all that liquid splashing around in Newt's stomach would only slow him down. Then again, Newt was already slow and had way too many freckles. Henchmen weren't supposed to have freckles.

But Newt was better than nothing. He was loyal. He was trustworthy. And at least one of his freckles looked like a large rat, or maybe a kitten. No, definitely a rat.

Taking a deep breath, Zachary waited for the parade to start. Every year the mayor led the way, waving and smiling, with cars, bands, and parade marchers following behind. It was tradition.

But this year tradition would be broken. Zachary and Newt were two of the only people in Plentyville who knew why: Zachary had turned the mayor into a brain-eating zombie.

Last week, Zachary and Mayor Mudfogg had battled to see who would be invited to join the Society of Utterly Rotten, Beastly, and Loathsome Lawbreaking Scoundrels, better known as SOURBALLS. But in the end, Zachary came away empty-handed while the mayor, with his fried zombie brain, was left empty-headed.

Zachary closed his eyes. He imagined himself flying off in the SOURBALLS evil blimp and living in their Fortress of Mayhem. He pictured helping them perform evil schemes like turning the moon into sausage patties, squashing Saint Louis with a giant bagel, or letting loose

OH NO!

a swarm of man-eating muffins.

His stomach growled. He hadn't had breakfast that morning.

But while he may have missed his chance to join SOURBALLS, Zachary hadn't given up hope. Someday he would join their Legions of Destruction. Eventually, the world would fear his name! But he needed to be ready. So he practiced his evil cackle, hatched rotten plans, and performed terrible deeds.

Which was why he needed the 1,000 tired female crickets.

Zachary and Newt sat on the curb, only a few steps from the beginning of the parade. Zachary didn't think it would last long this year.

"Why did we need the crickets again?" asked Newt between Super Guzzle slurps and eyelid twitches.

"You'll see," said Zachary, smiling.

7

Newt took another huge gulp, and then belched. "When are you leaving?"

"In three days. I'll be gone all summer."

"I wish I could go," said Newt.

Zachary grimaced. "I wouldn't wish my fate on anyone. Although I could use a henchman to help me when I get to . . . I get to . . ." Zachary couldn't say it. It was just too horrible. He buried his face in his hands, a guttural moan trickling out.

"What are you doing here, Ruthless?" said a voice behind them. Zachary swallowed his sobs and turned to see Amanda Goodbar sneering with her narrowed eyebrows and her wrinkly forehead. Although she looked downright evil, she was the biggest Goody Two-shoes in Zachary's school.

"I didn't expect to see you watching a parade," she said. "Shouldn't you be trying to turn kittens into blobs of snot or

something just as sinister?"

Zachary smiled. Turning kittens into snot wasn't a bad idea. He'd need to write that plan down for later. "Just looking forward to the parade, Goodbar." Zachary blinked. Since innocent-looking people blink a lot, Zachary's twinkling eyes were the perfect cover for his evil ways.

"Blink all you want, Ruthless. But you can't fool me. I know you're up to something."

"Who, me?"

"Yes, you," said Amanda. "But in a few days I'm leaving. I'll be gone from rotten kids like you all summer long. I can't wait."

Before Zachary could say anything, the parade began, and Amanda ran away to watch.

A team of police cars led the way, slowly rolling by with flashing lights. Zachary squirmed. Like most no-gooders, Zachary didn't like the police. Terrible deeds and police go together like peanut butter and onions.

Next, two convertibles drove by. A sign

on the door of the first car announced the winner of this year's beauty pageant. A bald man with a big handlebar mustache waved from inside. In the second car, a young girl with a crown blew kisses to the crowd. Her door read, FIRST PLACE, ANNUAL HANDLEBAR MUSTACHE CONTEST.

"Did you switch the signs?" asked Newt. Zachary smiled. It was the sort of small detail that separated true evildoers from evildoer wannabes.

A fire truck drove by next, blaring its horns. Firefighters threw bags of candy to the crowd. Kids swarmed onto the

FIRST PLACE, ANNUAL
HANDLEBAR
MUSTACHE
CONTEST

pavement grabbing the bags, giggling and smiling.

But Zachary and Newt didn't move. They waited: Zachary calmly, Newt jittering.

Next came the high school marching band. This was it!

Three tuba players led the band, followed by a host of trumpeters. Zachary leaned forward.

A girl threw a baton high in the air. Zachary's eyes widened.

The first tuba player tooted. A cricket jumped out, and landed in the baton twirler's hair. No one seemed to notice except Zachary. A warm feeling crept into his toes. Then nothing happened for a few seconds, and Zachary wondered if things would go as planned. The warm feeling in his toes cooled.

But as soon as the twirler threw her

baton a second time, the crickets came. Hundreds of them. They jumped from inside the instruments and onto horrified band members. They leaped down their shirts and into their pants, into their hair and onto their shoulders.

Instruments crashed to the ground. The baton landed on someone's ear.

Zachary grinned and then cackled.

Newt turned. "Do you hear a chicken being tickled?"

Zachary grimaced.

Meanwhile, bugs flung themselves into the crowd. People ran away, shrieked, and fainted, although not always in that order.

The parade came to a sudden halt, and those who couldn't stop banged into the people in front of them. The man with the handlebar mustache jumped out of his car, two crickets snuggled under his nose. The beauty pageant winner ran out of her car as well, three crickets on her sash.

Meanwhile, kids opened the bags of candy thrown

by the firefighters, suddenly realizing they were actually bags of live crickets.

Amanda Goodbar ran past, twelve crickets chasing her, a terrified scream trailing in her wake.

"Why did you need female crickets?" asked Newt.

"Females don't chirp," explained Zachary. "If we used male crickets and one woke up early, people might have heard it chirping. But as soon as

the band started playing, all the crickets woke up."

"I knew it was you." Zachary and Newt turned around to see Amanda Goodbar, panting and sweaty. Her wrinkly forehead looked even more rumpled, her limp hair even more droopy. "The jig is up, Ruthless."

"I don't jig," Zachary said. He knew that very few evildoers dance at all.

A cricket hopped onto Amanda's arm.

"Get it off! Get it off!" she screamed, and began jumping around in what looked very much like a jig. She shook her arm violently, and the cricket flew up in the air behind her, where it landed on a policeman's hat.

The officer frowned, looked down at Amanda, and grabbed her arm. "Rumpled forehead. Droopy hair. Sweaty ears. I think we know who caused all of this mess."

"But it wasn't me!" said Amanda. "It was him!" She pointed to Zachary.

Zachary blinked, and the officer smiled at him. "Nonsense," said the policeman. "Look at his blinking! Here, son. Have a souvenir police badge." He handed Zachary a shiny plastic pin that said SHERIFF'S OFFICE on it.

"But he's the bad guy!" sputtered Amanda.

"That's enough out of you," the officer growled.

Zachary smiled and walked away as the officer tightened his grip on Amanda. Soon, Zachary became lost in the crowd.

But where was Newt? Zachary glanced

back to the street. The police officer held both Amanda and Newt in his grasp.

Zachary froze, teetering between rescuing Newt and walking away. Eventually, leaving won out. He felt a twinge of regret for Newt, but just a twinge. After all, henchmen carried heavy moon-melting lasers, fed ravenous piranhas, and—most importantly—did anything to help the head evildoer escape. That was why henchmen made big money.

Of course, Zachary didn't pay Newt any money. But that wasn't really the point, was it?

No sense worrying about it. If Newt played it smart, he'd get away with a lecture and a slap on the wrist. Besides, Zachary had enough things to worry about. After all, he was leaving on his trip soon and had plenty of planning to do.

He was being sent to Good Samaritan School for the rest of the summer.